This Book Belongs To:

_____

_____

Benson's Birthday Surprise

July

					1	2	3
4	5	6	7	8	9	10
11	12	13	14	15		

It was Benson's birthday! So, he treated himself to a bowl full of berries.

None of his friends had said anything about his birthday, but Benson thought they must be planning a surprise party for him.

"When could it be? And where?" he wondered. The curious little bear ventured out to see if he could discover more about his birthday surprise.

Before long, Benson met up with Old Blue. Old Blue was the oldest and the bluest hound dog Benson knew. "What are you up to today?" Blue asked him.

"Just going for a walk, nothing special," Benson replied, not wanting to mention his birthday and ruin the surprise. "How about you?"

"Oh, I'm off to go fishing," Old Blue answered.

"Fishing? Blue would have been invited to my surprise party, if there was one," thought Benson.

Benson went on his way and soon spotted Timmy Turtle. Timmy polished his shell until everyone could see its shine from far away. Timmy was also so slow that he had to plan everything far in advance. If anyone would remember Benson's birthday, it would be Timmy.

"Hello Benson," Timmy said. "No time to stop and chat." He continued at his slow and steady pace past Benson.

"Where are you going?" Benson asked, thinking Timmy could be on his way to his surprise party.

"I'm going to town, Benson," Timmy answered.

"Did you need me to come along?" Benson offered. Maybe that's where his party was.

"No, you'll only slow me down," Timmy said and kept going.

Soon, Benson saw his cat friend, Fluffy. "How *purrfect* it is to see you," she purred.

"Oh? Were you looking for me?" Benson asked. Fluffy knew everyone and would surely know about his party.

"No," Fluffy replied, "but have you seen any birds? *Purrhaps* Rosey Robin? It's a *purrfect* day for bird watching."

"Birds?" Benson said, disappointed again. "No, I haven't seen any birds."

"I'm *purrfectly* certain I'll find one. Have a *purrfect* day," Fluffy said and she went on her way.

"Has everyone forgotten about my birthday?" Benson wondered. He was pretty sure now—his party wasn't anywhere. He was a little sad, but he could still celebrate his birthday on his own. Benson decided to go home.

Later in the afternoon, as he was enjoying his favorite honey sandwich, he heard the flutter of wings. There on his window sill landed Benson's little robin pal, Rosey. Maybe Rosey had come to take him to his party.

"Benson, could you please help me move my nest," Rosey asked.

"Oh," Benson replied, disappointed "Sure."

Benson went with Rosey to her nest. It held her two babies. He very gently picked the nest out of the big tree and followed Rosey to the new location.

Benson began to see balloons and streamers. Then, he saw all of his friends gathered with presents and a cake.

"Happy Birthday Benson!" all of Benson's friends wished him.

Benson was very happy (and very surprised) to see everyone. He set Rosey's nest on a low tree branch.

"Thank you, Benson. My little ones didn't want to miss your party," said Rosey.

Benson saw Old Blue. "I thought you were going fishing?" he asked.

"I did. Happy Birthday," Blue said and he handed Benson a gift-wrapped fish.